CC

C000156900

ME MYSELF AND US

THE NINE LIVES OF GABRIELLE: FOR THREE
SHE STRAYS - BOOK 2

LAURA MARIANI

PEOPLE
ALCHEMIST

ABOUT THE AUTHOR

Laura Mariani is an Author, Speaker and Entrepreneur.

She started her consulting business after a successful career as Senior HR Director within global brands in FMCG, Retail, Media and Pharma.

Laura is incredibly passionate about helping other women to break through barriers limiting their personal and/or professional fulfilment.

Her best selling nonfiction *STOP IT! It is all in your head* and the *THINK, LOOK & ACT THE PART* series have been described as success and transformation 101.

She is a Fellow of the Chartered Institute of Personnel & Development (FCIPD), Fellow of the Australian Human Resources Institute (FAHRI), Fellow of the Institute of Leadership & Management (FInstLM), Member of the Society of Human Resources Management (SHRM) and Member of the Change Institute.

She is based in London, England with a strong penchant for travel and visiting new places.

She is a food lover, ballet fanatic, passionate about music, art, theatre. She likes painting and drawing (for self-expression not selling but hey, you never know...), tennis, rugby, and of course fashion (the Pope is Catholic after all).

www.thepeoplealchemist.com
@PeopleAlchemist
instagram.com/lauramariani_author

NEW FICTION OUT 12 JULY

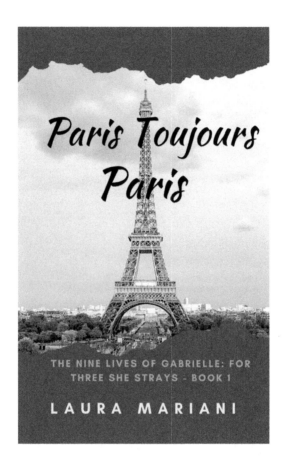

Paris Toujours Paris

THE NINE LIVES OF GABRIELLE: FOR
THREE SHE STRAYS - BOOK 1

LAURA MARIANI

ALSO OUT 12 JULY

THE NINE LIVES OF GABRIELLE:
FOR THREE SHE STRAYS - BOOK 3

Freedom
over Me

LAURA MARIANI

NEW NON-FICTION BY LAURA MARIANI

INCREDIBLY INSPIRING!
A BOOK PERFECT FOR WOMEN IN BUSINESS.

90 DAYS TO REBOOT YOUR CAREER

How to reinvent yourself, your career and your life

BY LAURA MARIANI

ALSO BY LAURA MARIANI

Fiction

For Three She Plays - Book 1 - 3

A New York Adventure

Troubled after the break-up of a long term relationship, Gabrielle sets out for a sabbatical in New York.

A travelogue searching for self, pleasure and fun. And the Big Apple doesn't disappoint.

Searching for Goren

Why are we always choosing people who don't allow intimacy? Is it because deep down we don't want it?

Tasting Freedom

As her trip to New York comes to an end, her shackles bare falling and Gabrielle begins to taste, finally, freedom.

Non-Fiction

STOP IT! It is all in your head

The RULE BOOK to Smash The infamous glass ceiling - For women & young women everywhere — personal transformation & success 101.

The Think, Look & Act The Part Series.

Think The Part

Upgrade your consciousness and mind-set. Make winning a key part of your life and business.

Look The Part

Upgrade your personal brand. Make presenting your unique Best Self a key part of your life and business.

Act The Part

A personal coach to act in spite of fear, right here, right now.

More non-fiction books and courses are coming soon. For new releases, giveaways and pre-release specials check www.thepeoplealchemist.com

You can also buy my books and courses directly from me at www.payhip.com/LauraMariani

ThePeopleAlchemist Press publishes self help, inspirational and transformational books, resources and products to help #TheWomanAlchemist in every woman to change her life / career and transmute any circumstance into gold, a bit like magic to **Unlock Ignite Transform.**

ISBN: 978-1-915501-12-7

ME MYSELF AND US

" 'What are you afraid of?' he asked.

'Losing control.' I replied.

'Sometimes losing control can be wicked awesome.' He said.

' And sometimes it's a disaster.'""

- WORDSAREPUREMAGIC

Gabrielle was standing in front of Mr Wonderful, looking at him looking at her. He was sitting at her desk by the window with a letter unfolded in his hands.

Gone was the loving look he had when she left for her walk.

The colour had drained from his cheeks. Instead, he looked stone-faced, almost grey; his eyes were red and swollen.

She couldn't understand what had happened in such a short time when she suddenly noticed the open drawer where she kept THE letter from *Le PDG.*

Before meeting *Le PDG*, Gabrielle was a provincial middle-class girl who, against the odds, had made it in the oppressively male-dominated world.

He opened her up to sexual and emotional freedom she had never before experienced.

But, this time, she was the other woman, breaking her values to meet her needs.

After her New York trip, Paris promised more freedom.
Instead, it raised more bonds to break ...

"Dear Gabrielle,

Don't be afraid of how much I desire you. I will shield you with love the next time I see you, with kisses and caresses.

I want to dive with you in all the pleasures of the flesh so that you faint.

I want you to be astounded by me and admit that you have never dreamed of such a thing possible ...

And then, when you are old, I want you to remember and tremble with pleasure when you think of me.

You make me hotter than hell... everything you do gets me hotter than hell.

You have raised new hope and fun in me, and I love you, your pussy hair I felt with my fingers, the inside of your pussy, hot and wet I felt with my fingers...

All this madness I asked of you, I know there is confusion in your silence — but there are no actual words to describe my great love....

Last night I dreamed about you; I do not know what occurred exactly. What I do know is that we kept fusing into one another. I was you. You were me.

Then, we caught fire. I remember I was smothering the fire with my shirt. But you were a different, a shadow, as drawn with chalk, and you were lifeless, fading away from me.

Please don't leave me, my darling Gabrielle. I am nothing without you."

Her cheeks went bright red, not knowing what to say. Sheepishly, she hoped that he hadn't read that far or couldn't quite grasp what the letter said. After all, Mr Wonderful's French was pretty basic …

But the look on his face told otherwise: somehow, he managed it and undoubtedly got the gist. He was sitting there, motionless and speechless. He didn't greet or hug her as he usually would have.

She knew she was in trouble. Paris, Toujours, Paris still taunting her.

Le PDG wrote that letter to her when he feared that their love affair would end soon.

It happened just after the annual Global strategy conference in *Londrienne.*

All board directors of the different companies worldwide attend the meeting as it is customs. *Le PDG* had kept the company headquarters there, just where his grandfather founded it.

The Group had now reached such a humongous proportion that they were struggling to find rooms for everyone in the only three hotels in the small town.

Many were staying in the adjacent cities, and buses had to be arranged to transport people back and forward to the three days conference. Same for the taxis: there were only two privately owned ones in town, and her PA booked one for her way in advance to ensure she could get around.

"*Bonjour Madame*", the taxi driver greeted her.

"*Nous sommes occupés, très occupés. Tout le monde et sa sœur sont venus au Vatican pour voir le Pape*", he said smiling,

making the comparison between the company and *Le PDG* and Vatican City and the Pope.

This town reminded her of her childhood: her *Mamie* was French and had a house in a small village in Provence.

So Gabrielle and her parents used to spend every summer there. Although the two towns were in opposite directions, one in the North and the other in the south of France, the similarities were striking, as with most small French villages.

The love of a long mid-afternoon break and a slower pace of life is perhaps one of the reasons why living in France sounds idyllic to everybody outside France who wants to leave the city frenzy behind.

The pint-size suburb, however, made Gabrielle feel even smaller. Always did.

"Come to think of it," she thought, "the same could be said for the English place I grew up in".

Different country, same cage.

. . .

When she moved to London, it was like shredding too tight-fitting skin.

She was glad the her role was based in Paris rather than in *Londrienne*. There were only 10,000 inhabitants, one cinema and one theatre: she would go crazy living there. Moreover, everybody knew everybody; most people in town worked for the company or were connected with it.

When she was little, Paris was her dream city, and now she enjoyed the London-Paris Monday to Friday exchange.

There were some definite pluses of living in Paris: for example, even on basic salaries, you can afford to eat at *chich cafes*, try new dishes and chat for hours, a champagne lifestyle on a lemonade budget, so to speak.

She was renting a one-bedroom flat in the centre of Paris, just a few minutes from *Gare du Nord* railway station.

It overlooked some hot new restaurants in town, with lots of mismatched furniture, ping-pong tables, fantastic art and an impressive courtyard. She could watch some of the Paris hipsters milling around while cooking.

. . .

The flat was beautiful with floor-to-ceiling windows and white walls, yet rent was cheaper than in London, helping to absorb the cost of her commute.

Every Monday morning, she would get up at 6 am in London to catch the 7 am train to Paris.

She discovered that by booking her Eurostar tickets three months in advance, she could get them for € 69 in return, not much more than double a weekly travel card in London.

She would get into the *Gare du Nord* just after 10.30 am, and after a few minutes on the *Metro*, she would be in the office.

From Monday to Thursday night, she would stay at the Paris apartment and keep her work wardrobe there to save on packing. By Friday afternoon, she was ready to return to London life.

Unlike on the Tube, nobody pushes past you on the *Metro*, which also always seemed to work. Being stressed and rushed is not the Parisian thing to do. Instead, you take time to admire the surroundings and taste the *café crème*.

Overall, Gabrielle was amazed at how straightforward this arrangement had been. Her mother was upset she was further away, while her father, far more laid back, was happy whatever she was doing.

. . .

Her London friends found it more difficult because she had minimal time to spend with them.

Living in two cities wasn't tough if it weren't for *Le PDG.*

She had travelled from Paris with the *TGV* for the annual Global conference; many others were doing the same.

The *TGV*, even first-class, was surprisingly cheap compared to railway ticket prices in the UK. It felt like the company had taken over the train.

Gabrielle had been working closely for months with the various people organising the event as part of her new branding strategy. Everything was planned for the millisecond.

She was anxious about seeing *Le PDG* with everybody there.

She had been practising her professional face in front of the mirror because she didn't trust herself. Her feelings for him. And his wife would be there. AND his children were attending the informal dinner.

Gabrielle was trying not to think about it.
    And then it happened, just like that.

· · ·

She was going over the last-minute details with the events team in the main conference room when she felt the need to turn around.

There they were: *Le PDG* and his wife.

He was showing her around, explaining the order of the day and evening, and making her feel comfortable. But, of course, she had to have her "game on", the dutiful supportive wife of the dazzling *Président* of the company.

Nathalie was tall, slender, and blonde, with long straight hair, dressed too old for her age. They had been childhood sweethearts, and she was only in her early forties.

Le PDG noticed Gabrielle was there and moved toward her to introduce them. He didn't want to, but he had to. He had just introduced *Nathalie* to everyone else in the room and couldn't avoid Gabrielle.

"How do you do?" *Nathalie* said in a charming accented English.

The two women shook hands. Her grip was firm, resolute as to say,
'I know who you are, and it won't make any difference. He will never leave me'.

· · ·

Maybe she was, or perhaps it was Gabrielle's paranoia and jealousy. She had no right to feel jealous. She was the mistress.

"What a difference from before ..." she thought.

She found out she was the bit on the side six months after she had split up with The Stud, after coming across a charity website that showed the picture of a couple who had a very successful fundraising event-
The Stud and his girlfriend.

The problem was that the fundraising event occurred when Gabrielle and The Stud were, allegedly, still together.

She had been the other woman, unknowingly and unwillingly so.

Gabrielle was S-I-C-K sitting in her bath, scrubbing and scrubbing for hours until she felt clean and remotely better.

She was so mad that she even dreamed of killing him a few times in the most painful way, then downgraded it to chopping his dick off.

But, THIS time, she was the other woman, knowingly and willingly.

. . .

And she experienced jealousy like never before. This time, she dreamed of killing the wife instead. Not him. Never him. He had made her feel alive like never before.

Before leaving the room, they talked a bit longer about the order of events. After that, the rest of the day was a blur. Gabrielle ran on autopilot.

She didn't see *Le PDG* again until the evening, at dinner. She took her time and care to prepare for the evening; she wanted to dazzle him.

Make him see she was the one.

She picked a little black dress, caressing her body in all the right places, revealing her slender but curvy frame.

"You are the curviest skinny girl I have ever seen", he told her once. "I love your ass".

He was a bum man, definitely a bum man.

The dress was showing off Gabrielle's assets, like the mounting of a diamond enhancing its brilliance without being too much.

"Perfect," she thought, looking at herself in the mirror.

. . .

Just a smidge of red lipstick as if she had bitten on her lips, and she was ready to go.

Her table was next to the main one where *Le PDG* was sitting with his wife, brother and sister and the other members of the main Board.

Gabrielle noticed he seemed distracted. He conversed politely at the table but kept turning and looking at her. He could not stop.

He wanted her, right here, right now. After that, he didn't care about anything else.

And when Gabrielle left her table to go to the ladies' room, he followed her there.

"You looked beautiful", he said.
    "I want you" as he pulled her into one of the empty rooms down the corridor and locked the door behind them.

"I want you. This is torture", *Le PDG* whispered.

"We can't. It's too dangerous," she said.

. . .

"I don't care". And, at that moment, he didn't.

He had had several liaisons before, but nothing like this. They were just unattached sex.

His wife tolerated his indiscretions as long as he didn't embarrass himself publicly. She knew he'd never leave her.

But this time, even *Nathalie* could sense something was different.

He had stopped his regular evening calls during the week and was distracted when they were together at the weekend. He seemed to come alive only when seeing the children and when it was time to return to Paris.

And he had started going back earlier and earlier.

He used to take the first TGV on Monday mornings. Then, it became Sunday evenings. And now he couldn't wait to leave just after Sunday lunch.

Nathalie knew something was wrong but didn't know what she could do.

Sex had never been her thing, and she was glad he had bothered less and less as the years went by. Travelling wasn't on top of her list either. She didn't have his intellectual capacity or depth and they didn't share many interests.

She knew instinctively Gabrielle was His One. She had to stop this.

Gabrielle could hear people passing by in the corridor outside. The fear of being found out added to the excitement of being in his arms. They had to be quick because he was due to make his speech soon.

They composed themselves and left the room one at a time. She waited a few minutes before returning to the main room; checked herself in her mirror, trying to catch her breath.

She got back to her table just in time to hear him speak.

After dinner, everyone mingled and chit-chatted away; Gabrielle played her part and circulated the room, ensuring everyone was all right.

"He looks so handsome", she heard someone say. It was a group of women working in the head office from the communication department.

"I'm wondering who is he screwing now? Poor *Nathalie*", one of them said.

· · ·

"I bet she lost count"; they all nodded.

"I think he is seeing *la Directrice des Ressources Humaines* right now, or so I have heard", she added.

"I'm one of the other other other women", Gabrielle stood there incredulous.

He opened her up to sexual and emotional freedom she had never before experienced. But, despite his claims to her being the woman in his life, that did not imply she had been the only one either.

She wondered how many had been before — even worse if there was someone else now.

Le PDG suddenly appeared from right behind them. The four gossiping women looked partly in shock, mortified and, most of all, terrified.

Le PDG had heard them. They disassembled and left with their tail between their legs.

Gabrielle noticed something else, though:
HE was the one looking terrified.

Not of what people were saying about him but of what Gabrielle was thinking. He could see it in her face. Her beautiful face was now turning away from him.

. . .

"Gabrielle, please don't leave", he said.

She couldn't bear to look at him and slowly but surely walked away. He could feel he was losing her, right there.

They didn't talk for the rest of the evening. Then, finally, Gabrielle made her excuses and left early. The event team had everything under control, and no one needed her.

But him.

Right now, though, she didn't care. She returned to her hotel room and lay there, staring at the ceiling for hours. Her mobile phone was buzzing from the myriad of texts and voice mails he had left.

Gabrielle couldn't talk to him. Neither did she want to.

"What have I left myself into?" she thought.
"Why did I ...?

The next day was the conference's second day, and she would have called in sick if she could.

But she had commitments, so she put on a brave face and carried on as normally as possible. She avoided being in the same room alone with him as much as feasible.

. . .

Le PDG, on the other hand, wanted to be alone with Gabrielle. Desperately.

He had to explain. Yes, there had been many before her. But they were just sex. There wasn't anybody else right now. There hadn't been anybody else since her.

Not since he first saw her, even before they had started being together.

He had to explain. Gabrielle had to know.

It was then when he wrote THE letter; he poured his heart and soul on paper.

" .... All this madness I asked of you, I know there is confusion in your silence — but there are no actual words to describe my great love....

Last night I dreamed about you .... We kept fusing into one another. I was you. You were me.

... But you were a different, a shadow, as drawn with chalk, and you were lifeless, fading away from me.

Please don't leave me, my darling Gabrielle. I am nothing without you.

I'm yours forever."

_____

"Yes, forever mine, forever hers", she thought at the time.

And now *Le PDG* was standing between her and the most amazingly perfect man she had ever met. Loving, open, available physically and emotionally, present and tender.

Now she was the one who had to explain to Mr Wonderful. Desperately.

"How to explain what *Le PDG* had meant to her and why?" she wasn't even sure she knew herself to the full extent.
    One thing was for sure. He had to know there wasn't anybody else right now. And there hadn't been anybody else since him. Or ever will.

Me, myself and us.

AFTERWORD

Intensity-seeking is an enslavement of our own perpetuation.

When we step out of the delirium of always seeking someone new, and meet the same old sad and lonely child within, our healing journey begins.

Exhausting ourselves with novelty is a defence against our deepest pain, one that we cannot outrun.

But once we stop and feel our losses, we can being our healing journey and be the authentic joyous person we were born to be.

- Alexandra Katehakis.

DISCLAIMER

Me Myself and Us is a work of fiction.

Although its form is that of a semi-autobiography (Gabrielle's) it is not one.

With the exception of public places, any resemblance to persons living or dead is coincidental. Space and time have been rearranged to suit the convenience of the book, memory has its own story to tell.

The opinions expressed are those of the characters and should not be confused with the author's.

AUTHOR'S NOTE

Thank you so much for reading *Me Myself and Us.*

I hope you enjoyed this novella as an escapist story, but perhaps you also glimpsed something beneath as you read. A review would be much appreciated as it helps other readers discover the story. Thanks.

If you sign up for my newsletter you'll be notified of giveaways, new releases and receive personal updates from behind the scenes of my business and books.

Go to www.thepeoplealchemist.com to get started.

Places in the book

I have set the story in real places in Paris and in a modelled fictional town in the north of France for *Le PDG* backstory. You can see some of the places/mentions here:

- Eurostar
- Gare du Nord

- Le Metro
- TGV (train à grande vitesse)

Bibliography

I read different books as part of my research. Some of them together with other references include:

The Artist Way - **Julia Cameron**
The Complete Reader - **Neville Goddard**, compiled and edited by **David Allen**
Psycho-Cybernetics - **Maxwell Maltz**
A Theory of Human Motivation - **Abraham Maslow**

Printed in Great Britain
by Amazon